D1422906

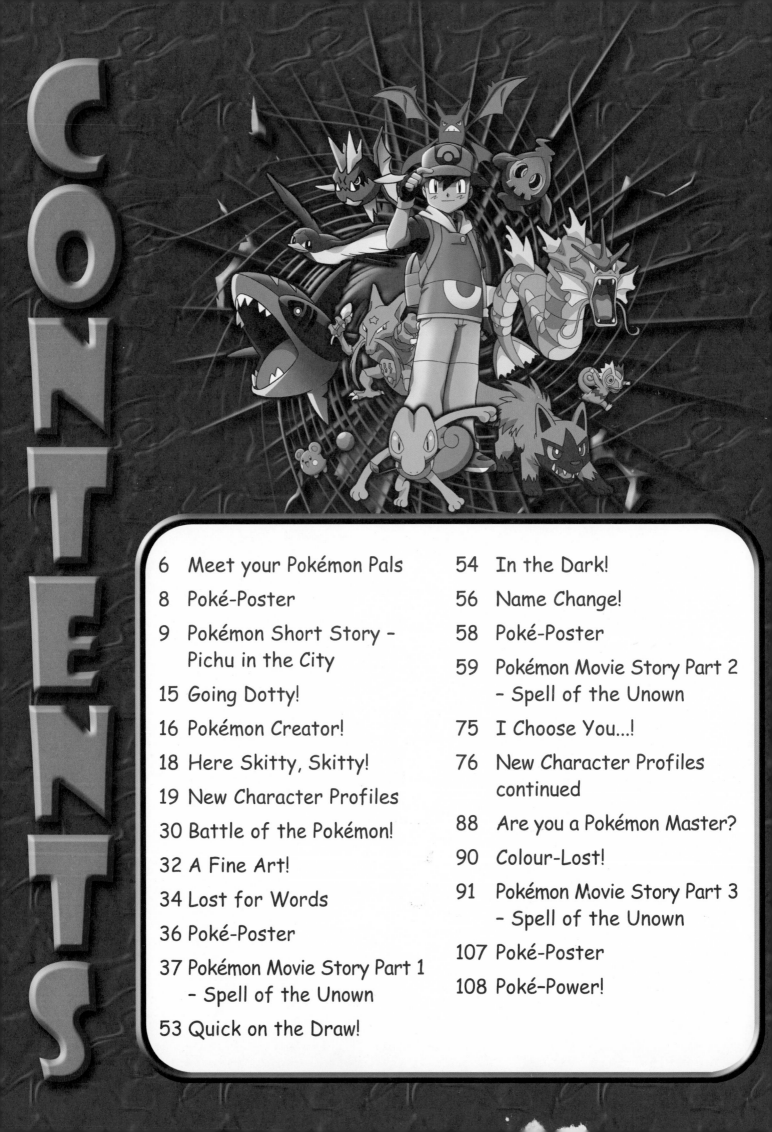

CONTENTS

Pedigree®

Published by Pedigree Books Limited
Beech Hill House, Walnut Gardens, Exeter, Devon EX4 4DG. E-mail books@pedigreegroup.co.uk
Published in 2003

© 2003 Pokémon. ©1995–2003 Nintendo/Creatures Inc./GAME FREAK inc. TM and ® are trademarks of Nintendo.

£7.50

MEET YOUR Pokémon PALS

ASH

Hot-headed and brash, Ash is a young Pokémon trainer who wants to fight as many battles as possible to become the world's greatest Pokémon Master!

MISTY

Misty is a fun-loving collector and trainer of Water Element Pokémon she's the best at what she does!

BROCK

Always with one eye on the girls, Brock is a breeder who raises the best Pokémon, helping them to discover their inner strength and personality.

PICHU IN THE CITY

Pikachu and his Pokémon friends were very excited! Ash, Brock and Misty had brought them along to spend the day in a big city!

"Now listen up," Ash told the Pokémon, as they rode a glass elevator up to the top floor of a tall building. "Just hang out here while we're gone. We'll be back at six o'clock exactly. 'Til then you can do anything y' want except get into trouble...Have fun!" After his friends had gone, Pikachu noticed two Pichu on the roof of the building opposite. "Pika!" he called, waving to them.

One of the Pichu, thrilled at seeing Pikachu, strayed too close to the edge, and almost fell off! Pikachu ran along a flagpole to call out a warning, only to be attacked by some angry Murkrow! SQUWAAAKK!

Pikachu lost his grip and tumbled through the air! Luckily he landed on one of a group of free-floating Hoppits, he then cleverly used them as stepping stones. Unfortunately, there weren't enough Hoppits to reach the other building and Pikachu dropped out of the sky again...! "Pika!" he cried in fright.

Meowth was working on the side of the building, washing windows - and he wasn't very happy about it! "When Jessie and James said they found me a job where I'd start at the top an' clean up, I didn't know they had *this* in mind!" he grumbled to himself.

He grumbled even more when Pikachu dropped heavily into his cart, catapulting him high into the air! "Waaaah!" he squealed, before landing back in the cart and shooting Pikachu to the roof where his Pichu friends were waiting!

PIKA!

But oh, no! How was Pikachu going to get back to the other building before six o'clock!?

Not to worry, the Pichu would help him!

They took Pikachu into an elevator shaft and through a vent that eventually led outside. They all dropped out of the vent, and landed - WHUUMP! - on the roof of a passing bus. "PIKACHU!" giggled Pikachu, enjoying the ride.

The ride didn't last long. When the bus turned a corner, Pikachu and the Pichu were sent hurtling off to land with another - WHUUMP! - on top of a sleeping Houndour!

"GRRRRRRRRRRRR!" growled the angry and rather annoyed Houndour, chasing after them over fences and through alleyways!

GRRRR!

Pikachu and the Pichu leapt over another fence, bounced off the stomach of a big, fat snoozing Snorklax and into the next alley. "PIKA!" laughed Pikachu.

The Houndour tried to copy them, but the Snorlax rolled over dreamily, and the Houndour crashlanded beside him! THUDD! Then to add insult to injury, the Snorlax rolled back on top of the poor, dazed Houndour, squashing him into the ground. OOOFF! It was just not his day...!

In the next alley, Pikachu and the Pichu stared at an amazing sight. It was a huge construct made from tyres, wheels, barrels and drainpipes, which swung up and down and around and around on ropes and pulleys.

"Pika?" frowned a puzzled Pikachu. Suddenly, lots of friendly Pokémon appeared. This was a wonderful adventure playground they had built, and they invited Pikachu to join in the fun!

All the Pokémon played and danced and sang - oh, what a great time they had! Then Pikachu noticed the time on the clock tower...it was almost five o'clock! Ash would be back soon!

Turning to leave, Pikachu found his way blocked by the angry Houndour, who chased him around the adventure playground! GUURRRRRR!! In the confusion, the Houndour accidentally crashed into the tyres that supported the rides. The adventure playground wobbled dangerously, threatening to collapse! "PIKA!" gulped Pikachu.

Working together, the Houndour and all the other Pokémon tried to save the adventure playground. A Magby welded things together, while a Hitmontop spun and kicked tyres back into place! At last, the adventure playground was safe again! "PIKACHU!" cheered a happy Pikachu.

13

But Pikachu now only had fifteen minutes to get back to the building before Ash! The Pichu gave him a lift in an old tyre, rolling it speedily through the streets, passed a crowd of people and into the glass elevator! GOING UUUUUP!

Happy but exhausted, they arrived back just as Ash, Brock and Misty returned! "Sorry t' keep y' waitin'," said Ash, on seeing Pikachu. "But we have a little surprise for y'!"

Ash led all the Pokémon into a large room, full of tables laden down with delicious party food! SLUUURRRP!

"Don't y' know what day this is?" Ash asked a puzzled Pikachu. "This is the day we first met...the day we first became friends. I think that's pretty special, don't you?"

"PIIIIIIKKKKAAAAACCCCHHHHUUUU!" a happy Pikachu cheered loudly!

GOING DOTTY!

Oh, no! Would y' believe it? I've dropped my Pokédex and smashed the screen! Can you see which Pokémon this is by joining the dots and putting it back together again? Afterwards, you can colour in the picture.

POKÉMON CREATOR!

Hey, Pokémon dudes! If you were pulled into Pokémon world, what sort of Pokémon would you like as a companion? Use your imagination and draw your ideal Pokémon. Don't forget to colour it and give it a name.

HERE SKITTY, SKITTY!

Meeoow! How many times can you find Skitty's name in this word grid? The names can be found across, down, diagonally and even back to front!

Y	S	K	I	T	T	Y	S
S	T	K	Y	S	T	K	K
K	K	T	I	T	I	S	I
I	T	I	I	T	Y	K	T
T	S	K	T	K	T	I	T
T	S	Y	K	T	S	Y	Y
Y	I	K	T	S	Y	I	T

NEW CHARACTER PROFILES

ABSOL™

Weight: 47.2kg
Height: 1.19metres
Type: Dark
Attacks: Scratch, Leer, Taunt, Quick
Attack, Razor Wind, Bite,
Swords Dance, Double Team, Slash,
Future, Sight, Perish, Song

AGGRON™

Weight: 360.2kg
Height: 2.11metres
Type: Steel/Rock
Attacks: Tackle, Harden, Mud-Slap,
Headbutt, Metal Claw, Iron Defense,
Roar, Take Down, Iron Tail, Protect,
Metal Sound, Double-Edge

ALTARIA™

Weight: 20.4kg
Height: 1.09metres
Type: Dragon/Flying
Attacks: Peck, Growl, Astonish, Sing,
Fury Attack, Safeguard, Mist, Take
Down, Dragon breath, Dragon Dance,
Refresh, Perish Song, Sky Attack

ANONTH™

Weight: 12.7kg
Height: 0.71metres
Type: Rock/Bug
Attacks: Scratch, Harden, Mud
Sport, Water Gun, Metal Claw, Protect,
Ancient power, Fury, Cutter, Slash,
Rock Blast

Weight: 68.0kg
Height: 1.50metres
Type: Rock/Bug
Attacks: Scratch, Harden,
Mud Sport, Water Gun, Metal
Claw, Protect, Ancient power,
Fury Cutter, Slash, Rock Blast

ARMALDO™

ARON™

Weight: 59.9kg
Height: 0.41metres
Type: Steel/Rock
Attacks: Tackle, Harden, Mud-Slap,
Headbutt, Metal Claw, Iron Defense,
Roar, Take Down, Iron Tail, Protect,
Metal Sound, Double-Edge

Weight: 1.8kg
Height: 0.20metres
Type: Normal
Attacks: Splash, Charm, Tail Whip,
Bubble, Slam, Water Gun

AZURILL™

BAGON™

Weight: 42.2kg
Height: 0.61metres
Type: Dragon
Attacks: Rage, Bite, Leer, Headbutt,
Focus Energy, Ember, Dragonbreath, Scary
Face, Crunch, Dragon Claw, Double-Edge

Weight: 21.3kg
Height: 0.51metres
Type: Ground/Psychic
Attacks: Confusion, Harden, Rapid
Spin, Mud-Slap, Psybeam, Rock Tomb,
Self destruct, Ancient power,
Sandstorm, Cosmic Power, Explosion

BALTOY™

BANETTE™

Weight: 12.7kg
Height: 1.09metres
Type: Ghost
Attacks: Knock Off, Screech,
Night Shade, Curse, Spite,
Will-O-Wisp, Faint Attack, Shadow
Ball, Snatch, Grudge

Weight: 1.8kg
Height: 0.41metres
Type: Water/Ground
Attacks: Mud-Slap, Mud Sport,
Water Sport, Water Gun, Magnitude,
Amnesia, Rest, Snore, Earthquake,
Future Sight, Fissure

BARBOACH™

BELDUM™

Weight: 95.3kg
Height: 0.61metres
Type: Steel/Psychic
Attacks: Take Down

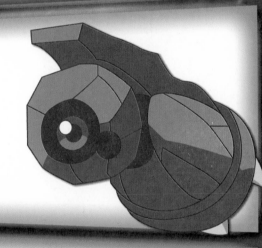

Weight: 39.0kg
Height: 1.19metres
Type: Grass/Fighting
Attacks: Absorb, Tackle,
Stun Spore, Leech Seed, Mega Drain,
Headbutt, Mach Punch, Counter,
Sky Uppercut, Mind Reader,
Dynamic punch

BRELOOM™

CACTURNE™

Weight: 77.6kg
Height: 0.99metres
Type: Grass/Dark
Attacks: Poison Sting, Leer, Absorb,
Growth, Leech Seed, Sand-Attack,
Pin Missile, Ingrain, Faint Attack,
Spikes, Needle Arm, Cotton
Spore,Sandstorm

Weight: 220.0kg
Height: 1.91metres
Type: Fire/Ground
Attacks: Growl, Tackle, Ember, Magnitude, Focus Energy, Take Down, Amnesia, Rock Slide, Earthquake, Eruption, Fissure

CAMERUPT™

CARVANHA™

Weight: 20.9kg
Height: 0.79metres
Type: Water/Dark
Attacks: Leer, Bite, Rage, Focus Energy, Scary Face, Crunch, Screech, Take Down, Swagger, Agility

Weight: 2.7kg
Height: 0.15metres
Type: Bug
Attacks: Harden

CASCOON™

CASTFORM™

Weight: 0.9kg
Height: 0.30metres
Type: Normal
Attacks: Tackle, Water Gun, Ember, Powder Snow, Rain Dance, Sunny Day, Hail, Weather Ball

Weight: 0.9kg
Height: 0.61metres
Type: Psychic
Attacks: Wrap, Growl, Astonish, Confusion, Take Down, Uproar, Yawn, Psywave, Double-Edge, Heal Bell, Safeguard, Psychic

CHIMECHO™

CLAMPERL™

Weight: 52.6kg
Height: 0.41metres
Type: Water
Attacks: Clamp, Water Gun, Whirlpool, Iron Defense

Weight: 108.0 kg
Height: 1.50 metres
Type: Ground/Psychic
Attacks: Teleport, Confusion, Harden, Rapid Spin, Mud-Slap, Psybeam, Rock Tomb, Self destruct, Ancient power, Sandstorm, Hyper Beam, Cosmic Power, Explosion

CLAYDOL™

CRADILY™

Weight: 60.3 kg
Height: 1.50 metres
Type: Rock/Grass
Attacks: Astonish, Constrict, Acid, Ingrain, Confuse Ray, Amnesia, Ancient power, Stockpile, Spit Up, Swallow

Weight: 32.7 kg
Height: 1.09 metres
Type: Water/Dark
Attacks: Bubble, Harden, Vice grip, Leer, Bubblebeam, Protect, Knock Off, Taunt, Crabhammer, Swords Dance, Guillotine

CRAWDAUNT™

DELCATTY™

Weight: 32.7kg
Height: 1.09metres
Type: Normal
Attacks: Growl, Sing, Doubleslap

Weight: 30.4kg
Height: 1.60metres
Type: Ghost
Attacks: Bind, Leer, Night
Shade, Disable, Foresight,
Astonish, Confuse Ray, Pursuit,
Curse, Shadow Punch, Will-O-Wisp,
Mean Look, Future Sight

DUSCLOPS™

DUSKULL™

Weight: 15.0kg
Height: 0.79metres
Type: Ghost
Attacks: Leer, Night Shade, Disable,
Foresight, Astonish, Confuse Ray,
Pursuit, Curse, Will-O-Wisp, Mean Look,
Future Sight

Weight: 31.8kg
Height: 1.19metres
Type: Bug/Poison
Attacks: Confusion, Gust, Protect,
Moonlight, Psybeam, Light Screen,
Toxic

DUSTOX™

ELECTRIKE™

Weight: 15.4kg
Height: 0.61metres
Type: Electronic
Attacks: Tackle, Thunder
Wave, Leer, Howl, Quick Attack,
Spark, Odor Sleuth, Roar, Bite,
Thunder, Charge

Weight: 83.9kg
Height: 1.50metres
Type: Normal
Attacks: Pound, Uproar, Astonish,
Howl, Uproar, Supersonic, Stomp,
Screech, Hyper Beam, Roar, Rest,
Sleep Talk, Hyper Voice

EXPLOUD™

FEEBAS™

Weight: 7.3kg
Height: 0.61metres
Type: Water
Attacks: Splash, Tackle, Flail

FLYGON™

Weight: 82.1kg
Height: 2.01metres
Type: Ground/Dragon
Attacks: Bite, Sand-Attack,
Faint Attack, Sand Tomb, Crunch,
Dragonbreath, Screech, Sandstorm,
Hyper Beam

GARDEVOIR™

Weight: 48.5kg
Height: 1.60metres
Type: Psychic
Attacks: Growl, Confusion,
Double Team, Teleport, Calm Mind,
Psychic, Imprison, Future Sight,
Hypnosis, Dream Eater

GLALIE™

Weight: 256.7kg
Height: 1.50metres
Type: Ice
Attacks: Powder Snow, Leer, Double
Team, Bite, Icy Wind, Headbutt, Protect,
Crunch, Ice Beam, Hail, Blizzard,Sheer
Cold

GOREBYSS™

Weight: 22.7kg
Height: 1.80metres
Type: Water
Attacks: Whirlpool,
Confusion, Agility,
Water Pulse, Amnesia, Psychic,
Baton Pass, Hydro Pump

Weight: 71.7kg
Height: 0.89metres
Type: Psychic
Attacks: Splash, Psywave, Odor Sleuth,
Psybeam, Psych Up, Confuse Ray,
Magic Coat, Psychic, Rest, Snore, Bounce

GRUMPIG™

GULPIN™

Weight: 10.4kg
Height: 0.41metres
Type: Poison
Attacks: Pound, Yawn, Poison Gas,
Sludge, Amnesia, Encore, Toxic, Stock pile,
Spit Up, Swallow, Sludge Bomb

Weight: 254.0kg
Height: 2.31metres
Type: Fighting
Attacks: Tackle, Focus Energy,
Sand-Attack, Arm Thrust,
Vital Throw, Fake Out, Knock Off,
Smelling salt, Belly Drum, Endure,
Seismic Toss, Reversal

HARIYAMA™

HUNTAIL™

Weight: 27.2kg
Height: 1.70metres
Type: Water
Attacks: Whirlpool, Bite,
Screech, Water Pulse, Scary Face,
Crunch, Baton Pass, Hydro Pump

Weight: 17.7kg
Height: 0.61metres
Type: Bug
Attacks: Tackle, Sweet Scent,
Charm, Moonlight, Quick Attack,
Wish, Encore, Flatter, Helping Hand,
Covet

ILLUMISE™

KECLEON™

Weight: 22.2kg
Height: 0.99metres
Type: Normal
Attacks: Thief, Tail Whip, Astonish,
Lick, Scratch, Bind, Faint Attack,
Fury Swipes, Psybeam, Screech, Slash,
Substitute, Ancient power

KIRLIA™

Weight: 20.4kg
Height: 0.79metres
Type: Psychic
Attacks: Growl, Confusion, Double Team,
Teleport, Calm Mind, Psychic, Imprison,
Future Sight, Hypnosis, Dream Eater

LAIRON™

Weight: 120.2kg
Height: 0.89metres
Type: Steel/Rock
Attacks: Tackle, Harden, Mud-Slap,
Headbutt, Metal Claw, Iron Defense,
Roar, Take Down, Iron Tail, Protect,
Metal Sound, Double-Edge

LILEEP™

Weight: 23.6kg
Height: 0.99metres
Type: Rock/Grass
Attacks: Astonish, Constrict, Acid,
Ingrain, Confuse Ray, Amnesia, Ancient
power, Stockpile, Spit Up, Swallow

LINOONE™

Weight: 32.7kg
Height: 0.51metres
Type: Normal
Attacks: Tackle, Growl, Tail Whip,
Headbutt, Sand-Attack, Odor Sleuth,
Mud Sport, Fury Swipes, Covet, Slash,
Rest, Belly Drum

Weight: 32.7kg
Height: 1.19metres
Type: Water/Grass
Attacks: Astonish, Growl, Absorb,
Nature Power, Fake Out, Fury Swipes,
Water Sport, Thief, Uproar,
Hydro Pump

LOMBRE™

LOTAD™

Weight: 2.7kg
Height: 0.51metres
Type: Grass
Attacks: Astonish, Growl, Absorb,
Nature Power, Mist, Rain Dance,
Mega Drain

Weight: 40.4kg
Height: 0.99metres
Type: Normal
Attacks: Pound, Uproar, Astonish,
Howl, Supersonic, Stomp, Screech,
Roar, Rest, Sleep Talk, Hyper Voice

LOUDRED™

LUDICOLO™

Weight: 54.9kg
Height: 1.50metres
Type: Grass
Attacks: Astonish, Growl,
Absorb, Nature Power

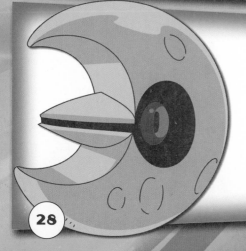

Weight: 167.8kg
Height: 0.99metres
Type: Rock/Psychic
Attacks: Tackle, Harden,
Confusion, Rock Throw, Hypnosis,
Psywave, Cosmic Power, Psychic,
Future Sight, Explosion

LUNATONE™

LUVDISC™

Weight: 8.6kg
Height: 0.61metres
Type: Water
Attacks: Tackle, Charm, Water Gun, Agility, Take Down, Sweet Kiss, Flail, Safeguard

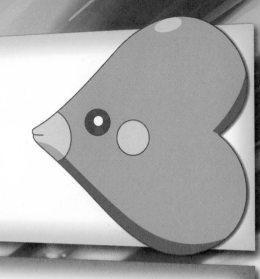

MAGCARGO™

Weight: 54.9kg
Height: 0.79metres
Type: Fire/Rock
Attacks: Yawn, Smog, Ember, Rock Throw, Harden, Amnesia, Flame thrower, Rock Slide, Body Slam

MAKUHITA™

Weight: 86.6kg
Height: 0.99metres
Type: Fighting
Attacks: Tackle, Focus Energy, Sand-Attack, Arm Thrust, Vital Throw, Fake Out, Knock Off, Smelling salt, Belly Drum, Endure, Seismic Toss, Reversal

MANECTRIC™

Weight: 40.4 kg
Height: 1.50 metres
Type: Electronic
Attacks: Tackle, Thunder Wave, Leer, Howl, Quick Attack, Spark, Odor Sleuth, Roar, Bite, Thunder, Charge

MASQUERAIN™

Weight: 3.6kg
Height: 0.79metres
Type: Bug/Flying
Attacks: Bubble, Quick Attack, Sweet Scent, Water Sport, Gust, Scary Face, Stun Spore

BATTLE OF THE POKÉMON

Uh, oh! James has challenged Ash to a Pokémon battle - and with these powerful new Pokémon they've both been training, it's anyone's guess who's gonna win!

ARENA 1

SEVIPER

V

COMBUSKEN

WINNER IS:

ARENA 2

SWAMPERT

V

AGGRON

WINNER IS:

How to play: This is a great game for two players. Flip a coin to see who's going to be Ash, and who will be James. Then for each battle flip the coin again to see which Pokémon will be fighting on your side. Take it in turns to write the first letter of your chosen Pokémon into one of the squares of the battle arena. For instance, 'S' for Serviper or 'C' for Combusken. Whoever links three squares in a row, across, down or diagonally, wins that battle! If neither of you succeed, that battle is drawn. Once one battle is over, go on to the next arena and do exactly the same. The trainer with the most wins is crowned the new Pokémon Master!

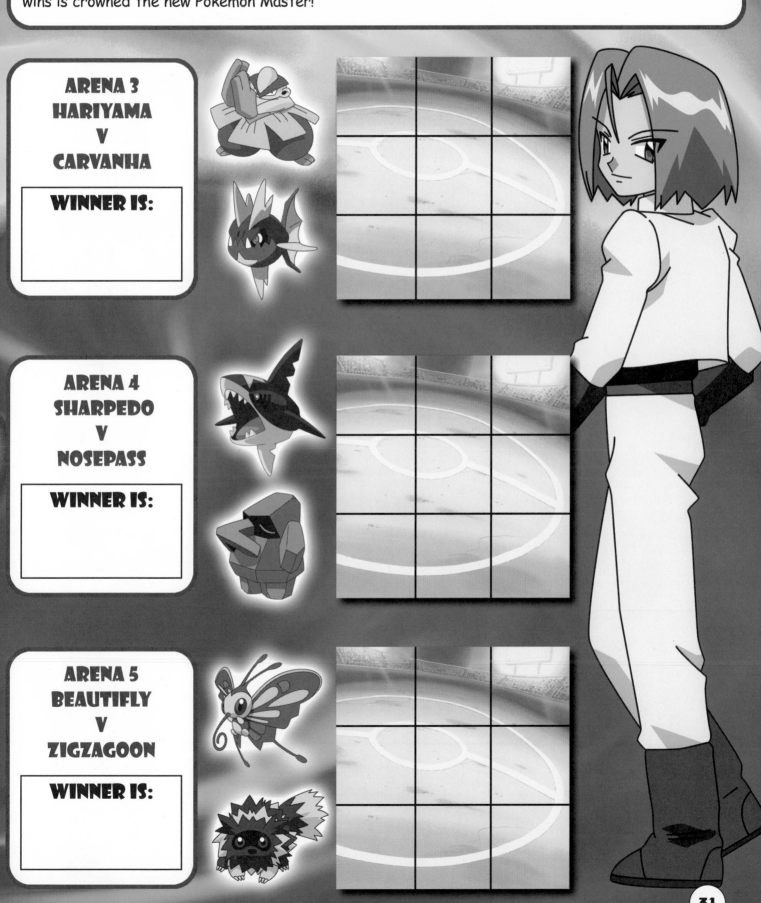

ARENA 3
HARIYAMA
V
CARVANHA

WINNER IS:

ARENA 4
SHARPEDO
V
NOSEPASS

WINNER IS:

ARENA 5
BEAUTIFLY
V
ZIGZAGOON

WINNER IS:

A FINE ART!

Using this picture of Ash and his Pokémon pals carefully colour the picture opposite to match.

LOST FOR WORDS!

Team Rocket here, frightfully needing your help! Can you help us find the hidden Pokémon listed below in that dratted word grid? The names can be found across, down, diagonally and even back to front!
One name is in the grid twice! And the remaining letters, reading left to right, spell out the names of two more Pokémon! Can you figure out who they are?

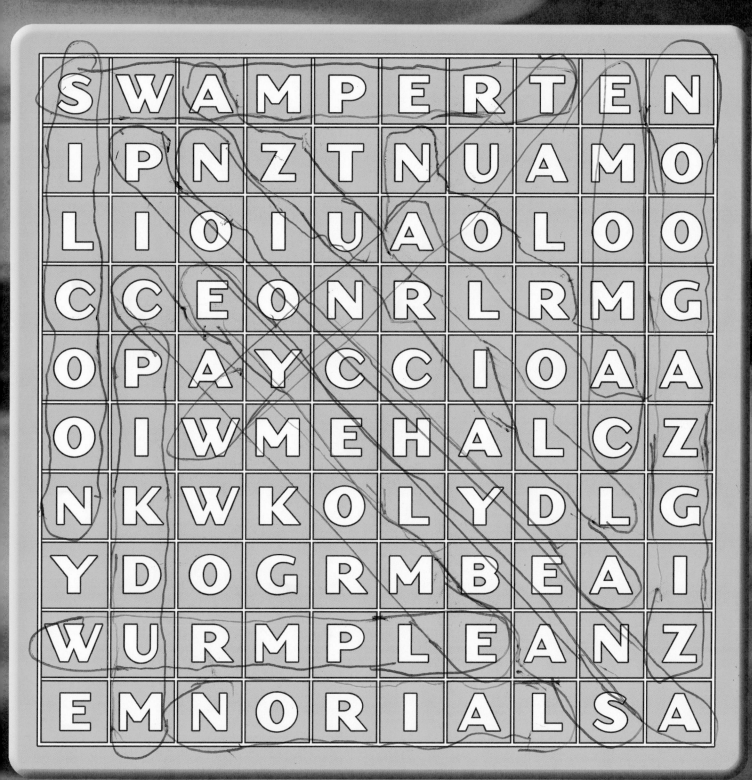

S	W	A	M	P	E	R	T	E	N
I	P	N	Z	T	N	U	A	M	O
L	I	O	I	U	A	O	L	O	O
C	C	E	O	N	R	L	R	M	G
O	P	A	Y	C	C	I	O	A	A
O	I	W	M	E	H	A	L	C	Z
N	K	W	K	O	L	Y	D	L	G
Y	D	O	G	R	M	B	E	A	I
W	U	R	M	P	L	E	A	N	Z
E	M	N	O	R	I	A	L	S	A

ARON
AZURILL
CAMOME
LAIRON
MUDKIP
NINCADA
POOCHYENA
SABLEYE
SILCOON
SWAMPERT
WURMPLE
WYNAUT
ZIGZAGOON

Which Pokémon name appears twice?

CAMOME

The Pokémon names from the remaining letters are:

TAILOW

KYGORE

The Pokémon name used twice is Camome. The Pokémon names from the remaining letters are Taillow and Kyogre!

THE SPELL OF THE UNOWN™

The town of Greenfield, and in the mansion home of Professor Spencer Hale, the Professor was showing his young daughter, Molly, a picture book of ancient Pokémon. One of the pictures showed Pokémon known only as the Unown.

Molly looked sadly at her father. "This is the one you're looking for, isn't it?" she asked.

Her father sighed heavily. "Yes...I've been looking for it ever since..." His voice trailed off as memories of his wife, Molly's missing mother, flooded back. He believed the Unown had something to do with her disappearance.

Molly pointed to another picture. "There's Entei!" she laughed. "He's big and strong...just like you are, Papa!"

Professor Hale laughed. "Well, I am Entei!"

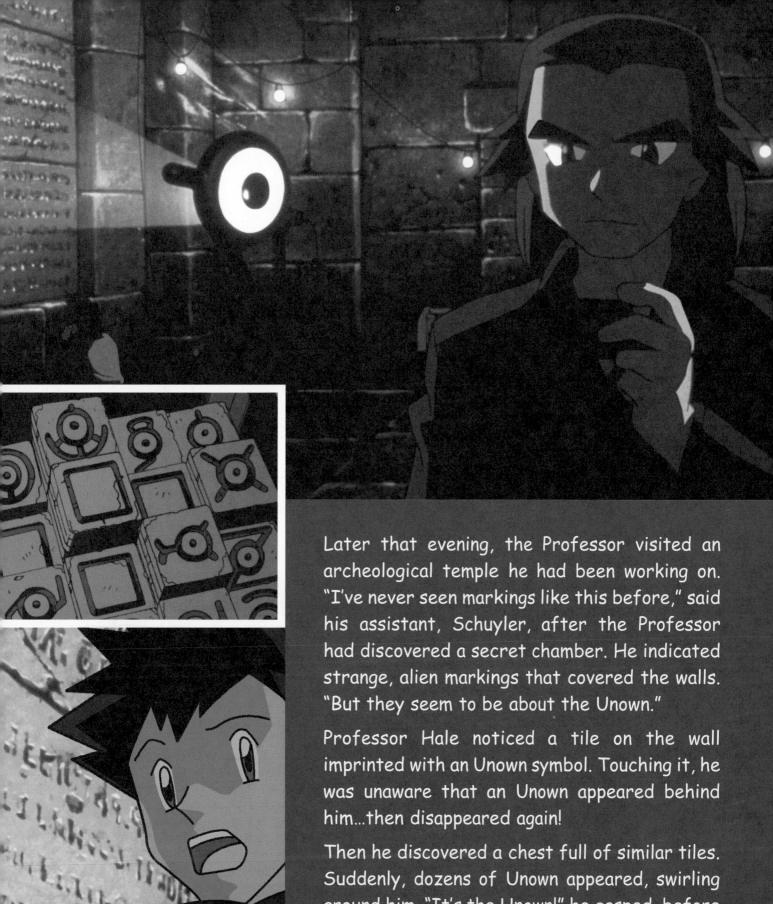

Later that evening, the Professor visited an archeological temple he had been working on. "I've never seen markings like this before," said his assistant, Schuyler, after the Professor had discovered a secret chamber. He indicated strange, alien markings that covered the walls. "But they seem to be about the Unown."

Professor Hale noticed a tile on the wall imprinted with an Unown symbol. Touching it, he was unaware that an Unown appeared behind him...then disappeared again!

Then he discovered a chest full of similar tiles. Suddenly, dozens of Unown appeared, swirling around him. "It's the Unown!" he gasped, before disappearing in a bright flash, falling down, down into a mysterious void, where the Unown danced and sang eerily around him!

Schuyler cried out in alarm when he realised the Professor had vanished. "Professor? Professor??!" he called out, helplessly.

Schuyler brought the chest and the bad news back to Molly. Distraught, she took the chest to her bedroom, using the tiles to spell out the names 'Mama' and Papa', her sad tears splashing on them as she did so.

From the temple chamber, the Unown emerged and flew to Molly's side. "Unown!" she gasped, as a powerful energy vortex swirled around them. "D' you wanna play with me?"

The ground beneath Molly's feet transformed to crystal, which spread like a tidal wave rapidly through the mansion, forcing Schuyler and the servants to flee for their lives! "Molly!" screamed Schuyler in terror, as the entire mansion was transformed into a crystal flower-like palace!

Molly's heart ached for her father. "Papa...please come back!" she sobbed, staring at a picture of the Entei in her father's book. Looking round, she saw the Entei forming inside the Unowns energy vortex. "P-Papa?" she asked, hopefully. The Entei nodded. "If that is what you wish," he said, in her father's voice...!

Elsewhere, Ash, Misty and Brock were continuing their travels, when they came across a friendly girl called Lisa, who also happened to be a trainer.

"Wanna battle?" she asked. Ash grinned. "All right," he said, pulling out a Poké Ball. "A work out'll help me stay in shape for the Johto League! Totodile, I choose you...!"

And the fight was on!

Lisa chose a Granbull, who charged at Totodile, only for Totodile to leap aside before blasting him with a Water Gun attack! SPLOOOSSH!

Lisa counter-attacked with a Girafarig, who caught Ash's Chikorita with its hyper beams, sending it sprawling in the dusty ground! But Ash wasn't finished yet. It was time for Pikachu to show what he could do!

"PIKACHU!" cried Pikachu, sending his Thundershock electric blast directly at Lisa's next Pokémon, Quagsire! Quagsire returned with his powerful water gun tidal wave, which sent poor Pikachu hurtling back! Then they charged each other, head-butting hard, before they both collapsed to the ground, feeling very dazed!

Later, after a hearty lunch, Lisa took the friends to the outskirts of Greenfield where stood a Pokémon Centre. "Greenfield's supposed to be a beautiful town, with beautiful gardens and a beautiful mountain with a beautiful mansion right at the top," Misty told Ash and Brock.

But what they saw was any anything but - - ! Spreading out from Professor Hale's mansion, the crystal wave was sweeping across Greenfield! As Ash and his friends stared at the sight in horror, a TV news team arrived to report on the bizarre phenomenon.

Seeing the report, Professor Oak and Nurse Tracey, and Delia Ketchum, Ash's mother, hurried to the scene. They had all known Professor Hale for many years. "He was my top student," Professor Oak explained. "In fact, he sent me his latest research...on creatures called Unown!"

Ash's mother was overjoyed to see her son again. "How's my Pokémon Master?" she asked. Ash beamed proudly. "I'm doin' great!" Back in Professor Hale's mansion, Molly saw Ash's mother on television. "Papa," she said sadly. "I want a Mama, too." The Entei nodded. "If that is your wish," he said, before vanishing...!

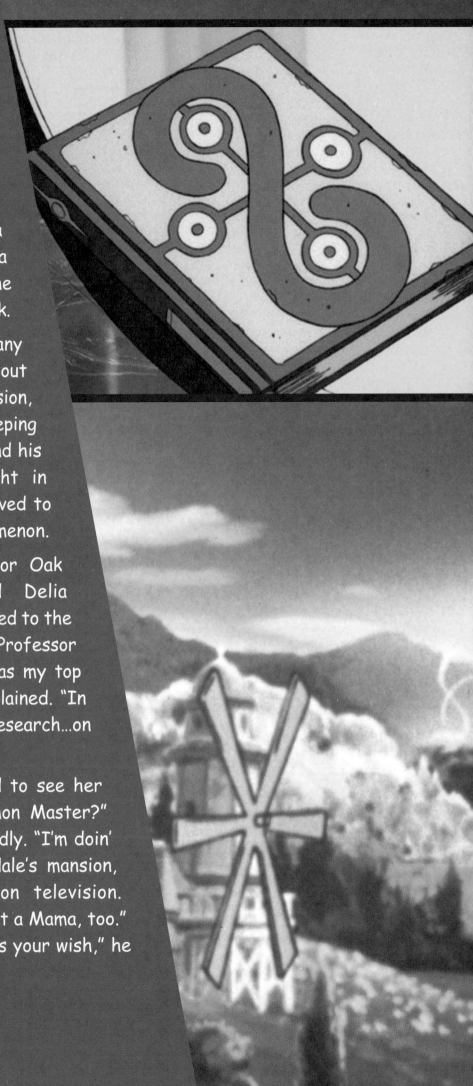

45

The Entei appeared before Ash and his friends! "I have come...for you!" he said, staring at Ash's mother. "You are...Mama!" The Entei's eyes flashed brightly, hypnotising Delia Ketchum. "Take me to her...take me...to my...child..." she gasped, before swooning across the Entei's back.

To Ash's horror, the Entei took off with his mother! "MOM!" he cried, chasing after them. "PIKACHU!" Pikachu grabbed hold of the Entei's tail and was pulled.

"Ash!" yelled Brock, pulling his friend back before he could follow. "Wait! You don't know what's out there!" Watching the Entei disappear back towards the mountain, a heartbroken Ash collapsed to his knees. "She's gone!" he sobbed, punching the ground. "I couldn't save 'er!"

Back in the mansion, in Molly's bedroom, she leapt up excitedly when the Entei returned with Delia Ketchum. "I have brought you what you wished for," said the Entei. Ash's mother woke up, looking groggy. "Mama!" squealed Molly happily, giving her a hug. Delia frowned. She tried to remember. "You called me...Mama," she hesitated, puzzled, staring at Molly. "Yeah," said Molly. "And I'm Molly...'member!?" Molly thanked the Entei for returning her mother to her. "I am happy...that you are happy," he said.

At the Pokémon Centre, Professor Oak downloaded Professor Hale's reports on a computer. "The Pokémon that took your mother was Entei," he explained to an angry Ash. "One of the legendary Pokémon."

Schuyler, who had joined the group, spoke up. "The other Pokémon must have had something to do with Entei's appearance. They're inside the mansion." Professor Oak sighed heavily. "You mean the Unown...the Pokémon you and Professor Hale were researching when he disappeared. I was afraid of that..."

Elsewhere, in Characific Valley, a resting Charizard watched the news report of Delia Ketchum's bizarre kidnapping. He growled quietly, thinking of Ash. It was time. Flapping his powerful wings, he took off, flying up over the mountains...

The police, who had arrived to deal with the situation, ordered a bulldozer to smash through the crystals that were sweeping through Greenfield. Ash and Pikachu watched the bulldozer drive forward, tearing through the massive crystal spikes. KRRUUNNCH! Suddenly, more spikes appeared, overturning the bulldozer! SMAASSH!

On Professor Oak's computer, an e-mail was received from an angry Molly! "Go 'way!" she screamed. "Leave us alone! Mama an' papa an' me just wanna stay by ourselves forever so stay away! Ev'rybody just leave us alone!"

Everyone looked confused by her words. "Did she say her mother and father were with her?" asked Brock. Misty stared at the Professor. "That couldn't be...you said Professor Hale disappeared, didn't you?" Lisa perked up. "An' what about her 'Mom'?" Professor Oak frowned. "Very

Ash had had enough! "I'm not gonna wait around anymore, Pikachu," he whispered, out of Professor Oak's hearing. It's up to us to save mom on our own." Pikachu nodded. "PIKA!" he agreed. Misty blocked their path. "Stop right there! I'm going, too!" Brock joined in. "You're not leaving me behind!" Ash choked. "Guys...you're the best!"

Lisa handed Ash a strange device. "If you're gonna do something crazy - at least take my Poké Gear. You can use it t' stay in touch with the Pokémon Centre. An' if Professor Oak finds out what you're doing, it won't be from me!" Ash grinned warmly. "Lisa...you're a real pal!"

QUICK ON THE DRAW!

Pikachu isn't very good at drawing, so could you copy the picture of his new Pokémon friend, Blaziken, into the grid below? Time yourself and see how long you take! Then colour him in!

IN THE DARK!

These Pokémon are so tough, they've scared their own shadows away! Can you match the shadows to their Pokémon? Which two Pokémon shadows appear twice?

Answers: Slakoth and Shroomish.

NAME CHANGE!

Just when Ash has been trying to learn all the names of these new Pokémon, Pikachu's played a joke on him and changed all the names around! Using a pencil, can you draw two lines from each Pokémon to the two blocks that will spell out their names correctly?

A

B

CATTY

PASS

PELI

DEL

LUDI

PPER

EDO

BEAT

C

Answers: A) Pooch - Yena, B) Peli - Pper, C) Sharp - Edo, D) Maku - Hita, E) Vol - Beat, F) Ludi - Colo, G) Nose - Pass, H) Del - Catty

POOCH

MAKU

COLO

SHARP

YENA

VOL

HITA

NOSE

SPELL OF THE UNOWN™ CHAPTER II

Floating high in the air in a hot air balloon, Team Rocket were spying on Ash, Pikachu, Misty and Brock as they set off towards the mansion. "Hey!" snorted Meowth. "It's the twerps... they're walking through a stream comin' from that wacky buildin'!"

On the crystal dome roof of the mansion, Entei watched the approach of Team Rocket. "What's that!?" spluttered Meowth, upon sighting Entei. James looked down nervously. "It looks scary! Do y' think it'll attack us?!" Jessie crossed her fingers. "It's probably...harmless."

Suddenly, Entei released a powerful energy blast, which tore through the balloon! KAA-BOOM! "Nyaaaah!" screamed James, as they fell out of the sky. "A sneak attack...it's not fair!" Meowth, as they disappeared through the mansion roof, agreed. "Yeah, that's usually our job...!"

"Did you make 'em go away?" asked Molly, when Entei returned to her room. He nodded. "They won't bother us again." Delia still held Molly in her arms. "Look, Mama," said Molly pointing to the television screen. "They're showing our house. It looks nice!"

Ash and his friends had reached the end of the stream. They looked up at a huge waterfall they would need to climb to reach the mansion. Releasing Bulbasaur and Chikorita from their Poké Balls, he cried. "Now...Bulbasaur, Chikorita! Use Vine Whip!"

THWIIIIIIP! THWIIIIIIP!

The Pokémon fired their Vine Whips to the top of the waterfall, wrapping them around rocks. One by one, Ash, Misty and Brock used the Vine Whips to carefully climb the waterfall - - one slip, and they would have fallen to their doom!

They found themselves...outside Molly's crystal mansion! They were still being filmed by the TV crew, and Molly, Delia and Professor Oak all watched the report being broadcast. "That looks like..." gasped Delia, waking from her hypnotic trance. "Ash!"

"I think that boy must be a Pokémon Trainer, don't you, Mama?" asked Molly, excitedly. Delia, hiding the fact that she had recovered, cuddled Molly. "Uh..yes," she said.

Meanwhile, Professor Oak had contacted Ash through Lisa's Poké Gear. He scolded him for going off, and then warned that the Unown had the ability to read the thoughts of other life forms.

"The Unown can create new realities - altering the world using thoughts and dreams," he said. "They may be tapping into the imagination of Professor Hale's daughter. The crystal fortress could be one of Molly's wishes...made real by the Unown!"

Following Ash's orders, Vulpix blasted a hole in the wall of Molly's dream fortress. Immediately, Totodile released a powerful water jet through the hole which the children rode on to get them into the building!

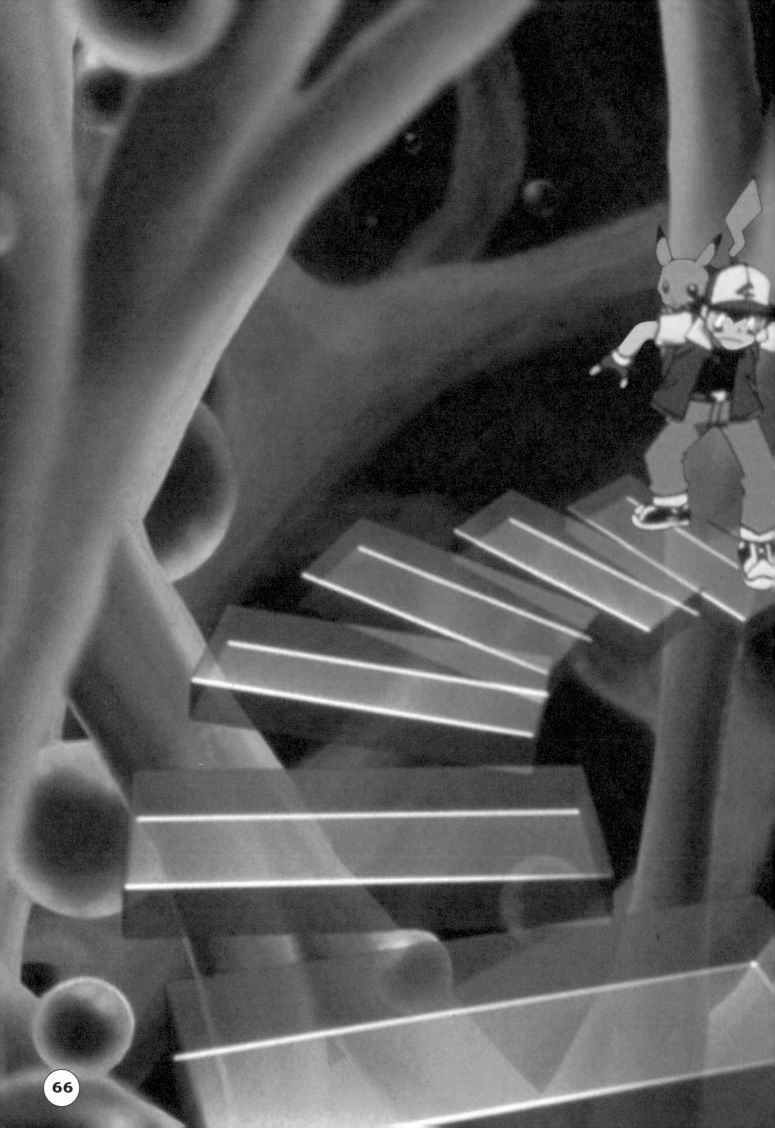

They found themselves in a bizarre setting, where large, red globules free-floated around them. They began climbing a staircase, only for reality to warp and twist, and the staircase became floating glass plates!

"Hey, what's going on?!" cried Ash in alarm.

"Maybe the Unown are creating a new reality," gasped Misty, as they leapt from plate to plate. "Just like Professor Oak said."

"Whatever it is," growled Ash, heading to the top. "We can't stop now!"

Team Rocket had also found themselves in Molly's dream fortress. They watched as Unown floated around a large room. "If we're quiet, we can sneak by them," whispered Jessie. "Come on!" James snorted. "I haven't seen this many strange letters since the last time I placed a personal ad!"

Molly realised that Ash and his friends had broken into the mansion. "I wanna be in a Pokémon battle, Mama!" she demanded, before falling asleep in Delia's lap. Entei sank through the floor. "You can...if that is your wish!"

As the Entei floated through the fortress, Molly appeared on his back, in crystal form. This was a body she had created out of her imagination - the real Molly was still asleep in her room! "Papa," she said. "Maybe I'm not old enough t' have Pokémon yet?" Entei merely replied, "You must believe you are." With these words, Molly transformed into a teenage girl...

Meanwhile, Ash and his friends had reached the top of the staircase and found themselves...in a beautiful grassy meadow! They looked up and saw Entei carrying Molly down a second glass staircase towards them. "Entei!" roared an angry Ash. "What'd you do with my mother?!" Molly stared at them. "The three of you're Pokémon trainers," she said excitedly. "Let's have a battle."

Ash ignored her. Entei! You took my mother! Now where is she?!" Molly scowled. "You're not any fun. There's no Entei, there's just my Mama and my Papa and me!"

"LIAR!!" screamed Ash.

Brock held him back. "Easy," he whispered; then addressing Molly, "By any chance, would your name be Molly?" Molly grinned. "That's right, Molly Hale!" Misty frowned. It couldn't be Molly. She was much too old! "Don't forget," said Brock. "This is Molly's dream world created by the Unown. They can make anything that girl wants come true...!"

Molly was beginning to get annoyed. "Are you gonna battle me or not?" she demanded, glaring at Ash. Ash reacted angrily. "Yeah!" Again, Brock held back his hot-headed friend. "Why waste your time battling him when you can battle me?" he suggested. Molly beamed "All right," she said, creating a Pokémon battle arena for them to fight on.

Misty realised what Brock was up to. "Let Brock battle," she told Ash, rushing him up the glass staircase towards the tower. "We have t' go and find your mom!"

"ZUBAT! I CHOOSE YOU!" cried Brock.

"I choose...Flaaffy!" squealed Molly in delight.

Zubat and Flaaffy joined battle, Zubat striking first with a Wing Attack! ZZZZKKK! Flaaffy retaliated with a Headbutt - WHUUMMP! - followed by a Thundershock Attack! ZZZZZKKKKOWW!

"Zubat, return!" cried Brock. He pulled out another Poké Ball. "This battle's just getting started. Go, Vulpix!"

Molly chose Teddiursa!

"A Teddiursa?" chuckled Brock, sweetly. Figure a cute Pokémon trainer'd have a cute Pokémon!"

But Teddiursa wasn't quite as cute as Brock thought! Molly commanded, "Dynamic Punch!", and Teddiursa walloped Vulpix all the way to the other side of the arena!

"Hmm," thought Brock. "Her dreamed up Pokémon're tougher than real ones!"

While the battle raged, Team Rocket sneaked past and up the glass staircase. "I don't like the looks o' this place. It's like a storybook invented by a five year old!" moaned Meowth.

On the arena, Brock was still trying to befriend Molly. "You're a great trainer, Molly!" he said. "If I want a chance at beatin' you, I'd better rock 'n' roll!" Brock chose the powerful Onix! "I choose Phanpy!" giggled Molly. And her little Phanpy struck the giant Onix so hard with a Rollout Attack, Onix crashed to the ground, winded! Molly had won the battle!

"I CHOOSE YOU...!"

Which Pokémon are emerging from these six Poké Balls? Write your answers in the spaces provided.

Azurill

Taillow

Absol

Treecko

skitty

Groudon

Answers: Azurill, Taillow, Absol, Treecko, Skitty, Groudon

Weight: 11.3kg
Height: 0.61metres
Type: Steel
Attacks: Astonish, Fake Tears, Bite,
Sweet Scent, Vicegrip, Faint Attack,
Baton Pass, Crunch, Iron Defense,
Stockpile, Swallow, Spit Up

MAWILE™

MEDICHAM™

Weight: 31.3kg
Height: 1.30metres
Type: Fighting/Psychic
Attacks: Fire Punch, Thunderpunch,
Ice Punch, Bide, Meditate, Confusion, Detect,
Hidden Power, Mind Reader, Calm Mind,
Hi Jump Kick, Psych Up, Reversal, Recover

Weight: 11.3kg
Height: 0.61metres
Type: Fighting/Psychic
Attacks: Bide, Meditate, Confusion,
Detect, Hidden Power, Mind Reader,
Calm Mind, Hi Jump Kick, Psych Up,
Reversal, Recover

MEDITITE™

Weight: 550.2kg
Height: 1.60metres
Type: Steel/Psychic
Attacks: Take Down, Confusion,
Metal Claw, Scary Face, Pursuit,
Psychic, Iron Defense,
Meteor Mash, Agility, Hyper Beam

METAGROSS™

Weight: 202.8kg
Height: 1.19metres
Type: Steel/Psychic
Attacks: Take Down, Confusion,
Metal Claw, Scary Face, Pursuit,
Psychic, Iron Defense, Meteor Mash,
Agility, Hyper Beam

METANG™

MIGHTYENA™

Weight: 82kg
Height: 39metres
Type: Dark
Attacks: Tackle, Howl, Sand-Attack, Bite, Odor Sleuth, Roar, Swagger, Scary Face, Take Down, Taunt, Crunch, Thief

MILOTIC™

Weight: 161.9kg
Height: 6.20metres
Type: Water/Water Gun
Attacks: Wrap, Water Sport, Refresh, Water Pulse, Twister, Recover, Rain Dance, Hydro Pump, Safeguard

MINUN™

Weight: 4.1kg
Height: 0.41metres
Type: Electronic
Attacks: Growl, Thunder Wave, Quick Attack, Helping Hand, Spark, Encore, Charm, Charge, Thunder, Baton Pass, Agility

NINCADA™

Weight: 5.4kg
Height: 0.51metres
Type: Bug/Ground
Attacks: Scratch, Harden, Leech Life, Sand-Attack, Fury Swipes, Mind Reader, False Swipe, Mud-Slap, Metal Claw, Dig

NINJASK™

Weight: 11.8kg
Height: 0.79metres
Type: Bug/Flying
Attacks: Scratch, Harden, Leech Life, Sand-Attack, Fury Swipes, Mind Reader, Double Team, Fury Cutter, Screech, Swords Dance, Slash, Agility, Baton Pass

Weight: 97.1kg
Height: 0.99metres
Type: Rock
Attacks: Tackle, Harden, Rock Throw,
Block, Thunder Wave, Rock Slide,
Sandstorm, Rest, Zap Cannon, Lock-On

NOSEPASS™

NUMEL™

Weight: 24.0kg
Height: 0.71metres
Type: Fire/Ground
Attacks: Growl, Tackle, Ember,
Magnitude, Focus Energy, Take Down,
Amnesia, Earthquake, Flamethrower,
Double-Edge

Weight: 28.1kg
Height: 0.99metres
Type: Dark
Attacks: Pound, Harden, Growth,
Nature Power, Fake Out, Torment,
Faint Attack, Razor Wind, Swagger,
Extrasensory

NUZLEAF™

Weight: 28.1kg
Height: 1.19metres
Type: Water/Flying
Attacks: Growl, Water Gun,
Water Sport, Wing Attack, Water Gun,
Supersonic, Mist, Protect, Stockpile,
Swallow, Spit Up, Hydro Pump

PELIPPER™

Weight: 4.1kg
Height: 0.41metres
Type: Electronic
Attacks: Growl, Thunder Wave,
Quick Attack, Helping Hand, Spark,
Encore, Fake Tears, Charge, Thunder,
Baton Pass, Agility

PLUSLE™

POOCHYENA™

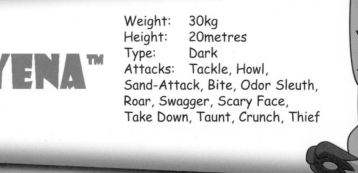

Weight: 30kg
Height: 20metres
Type: Dark
Attacks: Tackle, Howl,
Sand-Attack, Bite, Odor Sleuth,
Roar, Swagger, Scary Face,
Take Down, Taunt, Crunch, Thief

Weight: 6.8kg
Height: 0.41metres
Type: Psychic
Attacks: Growl, Confusion, Double Team,
Teleport, Calm Mind, Psychic, Imprison,
Future Sight, Hypnosis, Dream Eater

RALTS™

Weight: 206.4kg
Height: 7.01metres
Type: Dragon/Flying
Attacks: Twister, Scary Face,
Ancientpower, Dragon Claw,
Dragon Dance, Crunch, Fly, Rest,
Extremespeed, Outrage, Hyper Beam

RAYQUAZA™

Weight: 175.1kg
Height: 1.80metres
Type: Ice
Attacks: Explosion, Icy Wind, Curse,
Superpower, Ancientpower, Amnesia,
Zap Cannon, Lock-On, Hyper Beam

REGICE™

Weight: 230.0kg
Height: 1.70metres
Type: Rock
Attacks: Explosion, Rock Throw,
Curse, Superpower, Ancientpower,
Iron Defense, Zap Cannon, Lock-On,
Hyper Beam

REGIROCK™

Weight: 205.0kg
Height: 1.91metres
Type: Steel
Attacks: Explosion, Metal
Claw, Curse, Superpower,
Ancientpower, Iron Defense,
Amnesia, Zap Cannon,
Lock-On, Hyper Beam

REGISTEEL™

Weight: 23.6kg
Height: 0.99metres
Type: Water/Rock
Attacks: Tackle, Harden,
Water Gun, Rock Tomb, Yawn,
Take Down, Mud Sport,
Ancientpower, Rest,
Double-Edge, Hydro Pump

RELICANTH™

Weight: 1.8kg
Height: 0.30metres
Type: Grass/Poison
Attacks: Absorb, Growth, Poison Sting,
Stun Spore, Mega Drain, Leech Seed,
Magical Leaf, Grasswhistle, Giga Drain,
Sweet Scent, Ingrain, Toxic, Petal Dance,
Aroma Therapy, Synthesis

ROSELIA™

Weight: 10.9kg
Height: 0.51metres
Type: Dark/Ghost
Attacks: Leer, Scratch, Foresight,
Night Shade, Astonish, Fury Swipes, Fake
Out, Detect, Faint Attack, Knock Off,
Confuse Ray, Shadow Ball, Mean Look

SABLEYE™

Weight: 102.5kg
Height: 1.50metres
Type: Dragon/Flying
Attacks: Rage, Bite, Leer,
Headbutt, Focus Energy, Ember,
Protect, Dragonbreath, Scary Face,
Fly, Crunch, Dragon Claw, Double-Edge

SALAMENCE

SEALEO™

Weight: 87.5kg
Height: 1.09metres
Type: Ice/Water
Attacks: Powder Snow, Growl,
Water Gun, Encore, Ice Ball,
Body Slam, Aurora Beam, Hail, Rest,
Snore, Blizzard, Sheer Cold

Weight: 4.1kg
Height: 0.51metres
Type: Grass
Attacks: Bide, Harden, Growth,
Nature Power, Synthesis, Sunny Day,
Explosion

SEEDOT™

SHARPEDO™

Weight: 88.9kg
Height: 1.80metres
Type: Water/Dark
Attacks: Leer, Bite, Rage,
Focus Energy, Scary Face,
Crunch, Screech, Slash, Taunt,
Swagger, Skull Bash, Agility

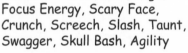

Weight: 1.4kg
Height: 0.79metres
Type: Bug/Ghost
Attacks: Scratch, Harden,
Leech Life, Sand-Attack,
Fury Swipes, Mind Reader, Spite,
Confuse Ray, Shadow Ball, Grudge

SHEDINJA™

SHELGON™

Weight: 110.7kg
Height: 1.09metres
Type: Dragon
Attacks: Rage, Bite, Leer, Headbutt,
Focus Energy, Ember, Protect,
Dragonbreath, Scary Face, Crunch,
Dragon Claw, Double-Edge

Weight: 59.4kg
Height: 1.30metres
Category: WICKED
Type: Grass/Dark
Attacks: Pound, Harden, Growth,
Nature Power

SHIFTRY™

SHROOMISH™

Weight: 4.5kg
Height: 0.41metres
Category: MUSHROOM
Type: Grass
Attacks: Absorb, Tackle,
Stun Spore, Leech Seed,
Mega Drain, Headbutt,
Poisonpowder, Growth, Giga
Drain, Spore

Weight: 2.3kg
Height: 0.61metres
Category: PUPPET
Type: Ghost
Attacks: Knock Off, Screech,
Night Shade, Curse, Spite, Will-O-Wisp,
Faint Attack, Shadow Ball, Snatch, Grudge

SHUPPET™

SILCOON™

Weight: 10.0kg
Height: 0.6metres
Category: COCOON
Type: Bug
Attacks: Harden

Weight: 130.6kg
Height: 2.01metres
Category: LAZY
Type: Normal
Attacks: Scratch, Yawn, Encore,
Slack Off, Faint Attack, Amnesia,
Covet, Swagger, Counter, Flail

SLAKING™

SLAKOTH™

Weight: 24.0kg
Height: 0.79metres
Type: Normal
Attacks: Scratch, Yawn, Encore,
Slack Off, Faint Attack, Amnesia,
Covet, Counter, Flail

SNORUNT™

Weight: 16.8kg
Height: 0.71metres
Type: Ice
Attacks: Powder Snow, Leer, Double Team,
Bite, Icy Wind, Headbutt, Protect, Crunch,
Ice Beam, Hail, Blizzard

SOLROCKS™

Weight: 154.2kg
Height: 1.19metres
Type: Rock/Psychic
Attacks: Tackle, Harden,
Confusion, Rock Throw, Fire Spin,
Psywave, Cosmic Power, Rock Slide,
Solarbeam, Explosion

SPHEAL™

Weight: 39.5kg
Height: 0.79metres
Type: Ice/Water
Attacks: Powder Snow, Growl, Water Gun,
Encore, Ice Ball, Body Slam, Aurora Beam,
Hail, Rest, Snore, Blizzard,Sheer Cold

SPINDA™

Weight: 5.0kg
Height: 1.09metres
Type: Normal
Attacks: Tackle, Uproar, Faint Attack,
Psybeam, Hypnosis, Dizzy Punch, Teeter Dance,
Psych Up, Double-Edge, Flail, Thrash

Weight: 30.4kg
Height: 0.71metres
Category: BOUNCE
Type: Psychic
Attacks: Splash, Psywave, Odor Sleuth,
Psybeam, Psych Up, Confuse Ray, Magic
Coat, Psychic, Rest, Snore, Bounce

SPOINK™

SURSKIT™

Weight: 1.8kg
Height: 0.51metres
Type: Bug/Water
Attacks: Bubble, Quick Attack,
Sweet Scent, Water Sport,
Bubblebeam, Agility, Mist, Haze

Weight: 1.4kg
Height: 0.41metres
Type: Normal/Flying
Attacks: Peck, Growl, Astonish,
Sing, Fury Attack, Safeguard, Mist,
Take Down, Mirror Move, Refresh,
Perish Song,

SWABLU™

Weight: 79.8kg
Height: 1.70metres
Type: Poison
Attacks: Pound, Sludge, Amnesia,
Encore, Body Slam, Toxic, Stockpile,
Spit Up, Swallow, Sludge Bomb

SWALUT™

Weight: 4.1kg
Height: 0.51metres
Type: Normal/Flying
Attacks: Peck, Growl, Focus Energy,
Quick Attack, Wing Attack,
Double Team, Endeavor, Aerial Ace, Agility

SWELLOW™

TORKOAL™

Weight: 80.3 kg
Height: 0.51 metres
Type: Fire
Attacks: Ember, Smog, Curse,
Smokescreen, Fire Spin, Body Slam,
Protect, Flamethrower, Iron Defense,
Amnesia, Flail, Heat Wave

TRAPINCH™

Weight: 15.0 kg
Height: 0.71 metres
Type: Ground
Attacks: Bite, Sand-Attack,
Faint Attack, Sand Tomb, Crunch, Dig,
Sandstorm, Hyper Beam

TROPIUS™

Weight: 100.2 kg
Height: 2.01 metres
Type: Grass
Attacks: Flying, Leer, Gust,
Growth, Razor Leaf, Stomp,
Sweet Scent, Magical Leaf,
Body Slam, Solarbeam, Synthesis

VIBRARA™

Weight: 15.4 kg
Height: 1.09 metres
Category: VIBRATION
Type: Ground/Dragon
Attacks: Bite, Sand-Attack,
Faint Attack, Sand Tomb, Crunch,
Dragonbreath, Screech, Sandstorm,
Hyper Beam

VIGOROTH™

Weight: 46.7kg
Height: 1.40metres
Type: Normal
Attacks: Scratch, Focus Energy,
Encore, Uproar, Fury Swipes, Endure,
Slash, Counter, Focus Punch, Reversal

Weight: 17.7kg
Height: 0.71metres
Type: Bug
Attacks: Tackle, Confuse Ray,
Double Team, Moonlight,
Quick Attack, Tail Glow, Signal Beam,
Protect, Helping Hand, Double-Edge

VOLBEAT™

WAILMER™

Weight: 130.2kg
Height: 2.01metres
Type: Water/Splash
Attacks: Growl, Water Gun, Rollout,
Whirlpool, Astonish, Water Pulse,
Mist, Rest, Water Spout, Amnesia,
Hydro Pump

Weight: 398.3kg
Height: 14.50metres
Type: Water/Splash
Attacks: Growl, Water Gun, Rollout,
Whirlpool, Astonish, Water Pulse,
Mist, Rest, Water Spout, Amnesia,
Hydro Pump

WAILORD™

WALREIN™

Weight: 150.6kg
Height: 1.40metres
Type: Ice/Water
Attacks: Powder Snow, Growl,
Water Gun, Encore, Encore, Ice Ball,
Body Slam, Aurora Beam, Hail, Rest,
Snore, Blizzard, Sheer Cold

Weight: 23.6kg
Height: 0.89metres
Type: Water/Ground
Attacks: Tickle, Mud-Slap,
Mud Sport, Water Sport,
Water Gun, Magnitude, Amnesia,
Rest, Snore, Earthquake,
Future Sight, Fissure

WHISCASH™

WHISMUR™

Weight: 16.3kg
Height: 0.61metres
Type: Normal
Attacks: Pound, Uproar, Astonish, Howl, Supersonic, Stomp, Screech, Roar, Rest, Sleep Talk, Hyper Voice

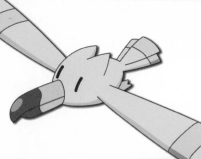

Weight: 9.5kg
Height: 1.9metres
Type: Water/Flying
Attacks: Growl, Water Gun, Supersonic, Wing Attack, Mist, Quick Attack, Pursuit, Agility

WINGULL™

WURMPLE™

Weight: 3.6kg
Height: 0.03metres
Type: Bug
Attacks: Tackle, String Shot, Poison Sting

Weight: 40.4kg
Height: 1.30metres
Type: Normal
Attacks: Scratch, Leer, Quick Attack, Swords Dance, Fury Cutter, Slash, Pursuit, Crush Claw, Taunt, Detect, False Swipe

ZANGOOSE™

ZIGZAGOON™

Weight: 17.7kg
Height: 0.14metres
Type: Normal
Attacks: Tackle, Growl, Tail Whip, Headbutt, Sand-Attack, Odor Sleuth, Mud Sport, Pin Missile, Covet, Flail, Rest, Belly Drum

ARE YOU A POKéMON MASTER?

Ever wondered if you've got what it takes to become a Pokémon Master? Answer the following Poké-quiz truthfully and find out for yourself!

1. In the midst of a fierce Pokémon battle, you realise you've run out of Poké Balls. Do you...?
a) Surrender!
b) Fight on and hope your Pokémon has the strength to win
c) Call a truce with your opponent

2. You're lost in a strange, dark forest at night. Do you...?
a) Start crying 'cos you're scared.
b) Make the most of a bad situation, settle down for the night and wait for morning to see where you are.
c) Phone home for someone to come and find you.

3. Which of the following Pokémon would you choose to train?
a) Beautifly
b) Groudon
c) Ludicolo

4. Your Pokémon start fighting between themselves. Do you...?
a) Hide until its all over.
b) Encourage them to see who's the toughest.
c) Tell them if they stop fighting you'll buy them all an ice cream.

5. Ash has challenged you to a battle. Do you...
a) Pretend you're not feeling well that day.
b) Train your Pokémon to be as tough as it can
   - this is one battle you're gonna win!
c) Suggest you both watch TV instead.

6. Misty invites you out on a date. Do you...
a) Blush, get tongue-tied and faint!
b) Tell her you're too busy training your Pokémon to waste time on such soppy stuff.
c) Buy her some chocolates, and a bouquet of flowers tied up in a big pink bow.

7. Your Pokédex is on the blink. Do you...
a) Forget all about it and take up another hobby instead
b) Demand someone mends it - NOW!!
c) Order a new one and wait patiently for it to arrive.

8. Team Rocket have you cornered with six powerful Pokémon - and there's no way to escape! Do you...
a) Grovel, and beg them to be gentle with you.
b) Snort loudly and growl, "Six against one? Ha! No contest!"
c) Suggest they take up Tai Chi to help sooth their troubled souls.

HOW YOU SCORED

MOSTLY A:
Call yourself a Pokémon trainer?? You are - - PATHETIC!! Hang your head in shame! You wouldn't last two seconds in battle! We've seen tougher worms than you! Go away and stop bothering us!

MOSTLY B:
Oh, yeah! You definitely have the potential to become one of the best Pokémon Masters around! Ash would be proud to call you his friend! Keep it up!

MOSTLY C's:
Look, you seem like a nice enough kid, but are you sure you want to be a trainer? Might be worth you thinking about becoming a breeder instead. You'd have a calming influence on your Pokémon and keep them out of trouble!

COLOUR LOST!

Team Rocket have been at it again! They've sucked all the colour out of this picture! Colour it in again and show them they can't win!

SPELL OF THE UNOWN™ CHAPTER III

Back in Molly's room, Molly awoke. Delia was looking at a picture of a beach in the book Molly's father had been reading her. "Mama," said Molly dreamily, looking at the picture. "I'm really glad you're here. I don't feel lonely anymore...I have a Mama and Papa now..." And she drifted off back to sleep...

Reaching the top of the staircase, Ash and Misty entered a room, and found themselves on a beach exactly like the one in Molly's book. Molly and Entei appeared. "I guess Brock couldn't beat 'er," Misty whispered.

Misty agreed to a Pokémon battle. She explained to Molly that she was a Water Pokémon trainer, and that she used to be the leader of a Pokémon Gym in Cerulean City. "Y' mean y' don't have t' be a grown up t' be a gym leader?!" said Molly, surprised.

With that, she changed from being a teenage girl to being one of Misty's age! "The real Molly must still be up in that mansion with your mother," Misty told Ash as he and Pikachu headed away. "Hurry up and find 'em!"

"I'll only use Water Pokémon, too!" said Molly, waving a hand. A huge tidal wave grew up out of nowhere, washing down over the beach. They found themselves deep underwater! To their surprise, they could still breathe! "I forgot," said Misty, laughing. "You can do anything you want to here!"

"C'mon!" urged Molly to Misty, unaware of Ash and Pikachu swimming away, with Team Rocket hot on their trail. "Let's battle! I'll pick first. I choose you...Kingdra!" And Misty chose...Goldeen!

Battle raged wild in the water! Thick, black ink erupted from Kingdra, blinding poor Goldeen! Thrashing about helplessly, he was unable to stop a sneak attack from Kingdra, who head-butted him hard, sending him hurtling away!

"Goldeen! Use your Fury Attack!" ordered Misty, but Kingdra was too quick! Evading Goldeen's strike, Kingdra struck again, knocking a breathless Goldeen to the ocean floor. "How am I doin', Misty?" Molly asked, desperate for Misty's approval. Misty smiled. "Not bad, Molly," she laughed

Meanwhile, Ash had finally reached Molly's room. "Mom!" he cried, seeing his Mom sitting with Molly on her bed. Ash quickly explained about Entei and the Unown. Delia shook Molly awake. "You'll have to know the truth," she told the little girl. "I'm Ash's mother. We have t' leave now, Molly!"

"N-O-O-O-O-O!" screamed Molly, and the room erupted...! Gigantic ice spikes burst through the floors, and Entei appeared, telling Ash to go and leave his mother! "Now she is Molly's mother!" he growled.

"That's what you think!" Ash growled back, throwing a Poké Ball. "Totodile... I choose you!" Totodile attacked with a water burst, which Entei easily evaded. He counter-attacked, bringing Totodile crashing down with a powerful energy blast from his mouth! ZZZZZZZZKKKKK!

Even more crystal spikes burst through into the room, almost spearing Ash! KKKKAAAAKKK! A bitter, icy wind swept around him as Delia begged Molly to stop the chaos! "Molly," she cried. "Think about your real mother and father!"

Ash knew there was only one thing for it! "PIKACHU!" he cried. And so it was Pikachu verses Entei, in a fight...to the death! "PIKA!" squealed Pikachu, releases a powerful Thundershock! ZZZZZKKKK! Entei retaliated with his own energy blast that struck Pikachu directly in the chest, sending him crashing down!

Team Rocket popped their heads up from the top of the staircase...and promptly opped them down again as an energy blast singed their heads! "What's going on?" emanded a frightened Jessie. Meowth groaned. "This must be a battle!" James roaned even louder. "And this must be a battlefield!" Together, they all screamed, AAAAAAAHHHHH!!!"

Entei's next strike was even worse! A huge explosion erupted - KAAA-BOOOOM!! - blasting out the wall, and sending Ash and Pikachu hurtling out into the night sky to fall...to their doom!

"Charizard!" gasped Ash, as he and Pikachu landed safely on the dragon's back. Charizard had arrived, just in time! He flew them back to the fortress, only to be blasted by Entei! ZZZZZKKK!

Again, Ash and Pikachu were sent hurtling outside, this time to be saved by the newly-arrived Misty, Brock and...Team Rocket!?? "You're the bad guys!" spluttered a disbelieving Ash as he was pulled to safety. Meowth snorted. "Uh, well," he said, embarrassedly. "If anything' happened t' you, we'd be outta show business!"

Ash pleaded with Entei. "If you really care for Molly...you have t' let her go!" Entei growled. "I will do as she wishes!"

Ash leapt back onto Charizard as Entei chased them outside, blasting them with a intensely burning flame thrower attack! HHHSSSSSSSSSSSS!! Screaming in agony, Charizard dropped through the air, smashing through the roof of Molly's room! Ash fell free, and Entei stood over the helpless Charizard, ready to deliver the killing blow...! "This will end it!" he snarled.

"Nooo!" screamed Molly. "No more fighting...Please Papa," she sobbed. "No more! I want things real again!" Entei stared at Molly. "I was created to be the father who could make you happy," he said. "If you would be happier outside...I must go!" The fight...was over...!

Or...was it??! In the secret chamber below, The Unown had created so much deadly energy, they could no longer control it! If Ash and his friends couldn't stop them, the whole world would be consumed! Reaching the chamber, Pikachu, Entei and Charizard blasted the Unown, time and again - ZZZZZZKKK! ZZZZKKK! - trying to break through the barrier they had created!

"Molly!" screamed Ash, with the battle going against them. "Y' have t' believe in Entei! Believe it can stop the Unown an' it will!" Molly screwed up her face and believed with all her might! "You can do it, Entei!" she yelled. Molly's belief filled Entei will awesome power...! He smashed through the barrier and blasted them, one last time! ZZZZZZZZZZKKKKKKKK!!!

The Unowns energies died away, and they were sucked backed into the Vortex...!
"I must go now, Molly," said Entei, disappearing.
"Just keep me close to your dreams..."

From out of the Vortex appeared Professor Spencer Hale, Molly's father...! And beside him...was her mother...! Her family had returned!

With the Unowns gone, Greenfield returned to normal once more. "You were right about Greenfield," Ash told Misty, as they stood once more on the steps of the Pokémon centre. "It is beautiful!" Brock laughed. "And it's real!"

"PIKACHU!" agreed Pikachu!

POKÉ POWER!

This is a game for as many players as you want - you can even play on your own! You will need one dice, counters, a pen and a sheet of paper.

Each players starts with 30 Poké-Power Points. Write this under your name on the sheet of paper. Taking turns, throw the dice and move the number indicated.

If you land on a square with either a plus (+) or a minus (-) sign, you either gain or lose the points indicated against your 30 Poké-Power Points. Watch the scores, because anyone who loses all their points is out of play! The winner is the person with the most points gained at the end of the game!

108

 -3

 +5

 +4

 -6

 -8

 +9

 -7

 +6

 -2

 -7

 +10

 +9

 -8

 +3

GAME OVER!

 -10

-4

 -9

 -5

 -6

 +1

 +8

109